For Sarah Louise

© ROBERT INGPEN 1986
Editor: Anne Bower Ingram
Designer: Robert Ingpen

First published by
Lothian Publishing Company Pty Ltd,
Melbourne, Australia
First published in UK 1986 by
Blackie and Son Ltd
Reprinted 1987, 1989
British Library Cataloguing in Publication Data
Ingpen, Robert
    The Idle Bear.
    I. Title
    823[J] PZ7
ISBN 0 216 92018 3

First American edition published in 1987 by
Peter Bedrick Books, 125 East 23 Street, New York, NY 10010

Library of Congress Cataloguing-in-Publication Data
Ingpen, Robert, 1936-
        The idle bear.

        Summary: Two teddy bears have a confusing time trying
to find out about each other.
        [1. Teddy bears — Fiction   2. Humorous stories]
I. Title
PZ7 1534Id   1987   [E] 87'1187
ISBN 0-87226-159-X

Typeset by Savage Type Pty Ltd, Brisbane
Printed in Hong Kong

Blackie and Son Ltd
7 Leicester Place
London WC2 7BP

The Idle Bear

Robert Ingpen

Winner 1986 Hans Christian Andersen Medal

Blackie
London

Bedrick Blackie
New York

"What kind of a bear are you?" asked Ted.

"I'm an Idle Bear."

"But don't you have a name like me?"

"Yes, but my name is Teddy. All bears like us are called Teddy."

Ted thought for a while, then said, "Well, Teddy, I have been Ted forever— at least fifty years, I think."

"Me too," said Teddy, "at least that long."

We could be related, thought Ted and Teddy together.

''We are related!'' announced Ted, pretending he had known for ages.

''How can you tell, Ted?'' challenged Teddy, ''How do you know?''

''Oh, I just know. Everybody has relations, I thin especially where I come from,'' said Ted beginning to wish it wasn't so.

"Where do you come from, Ted?"

"From an idea," said Ted definitely.

"But ideas are not real, they are only made-up," said Teddy. "You have to come from somewhere real to have realitives."

"Not realitives, relatives!" said Ted trying to hide his confusion.

Ted remembered that everybody he had met
had come from 'up the street', and said,
''I come from up the street.''

''What street?'' questioned Teddy.

In desperation Ted said, ''Up the street next
to your street.''

''What happens up the street?''

''That depends,'' said Ted , now really confused
''That depends on everything else that happens.
That should do, thought Ted.

"Like what?" demanded Teddy.

Ted tried to remember. "When I was young,"
he began, "I used to have a lot to do.
I was as important as a bear can be,"
Ted paused, then went on,
"later I was put away, and taken out,
and put away, and taken out, and put . . ."

"Put away where?" interrupted Teddy.

"In a box."

"What sort of a box? A bear box?"

"I don't know," said Ted, "just a box."

"Oh," said Teddy.

"Have you got a growl?" said Ted.

"I used to have one but it wore out," said Teddy.

"Mine still works," said Ted proudly, "at least I think it does."

"Don't you know?"

"That depends," said Ted, "that depends on what I do. If I stand like this it works sometimes.

Ted stood on his head as best he could.

Then he bent backwards.

"It's something to do with my tummy, but
I've never seen it," Ted said and stood
on his head again.

"It's a very small growl, Ted," said Teddy.

"It's better than a worn out growl," said Ted
feeling challenged again.
"It used to be very loud.
I used to be full of growl
when I was young,
up the street."

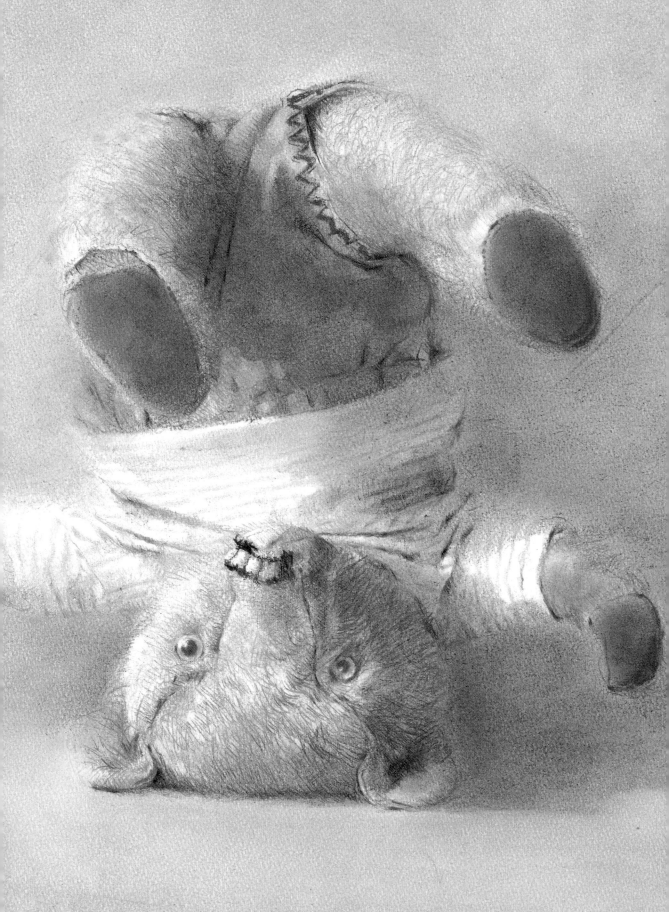

"I'm full of straw," announced Teddy.

Ted ignored that. It sounded reasonable and anyhow he was probably full of straw too, if they were related. But then scarecrows and cushions are full of straw and the thought of being related to a cushion annoyed him.

Ted was still thinking about cushions and scarecrows when Teddy startled him by saying, "Dogs."

"What about dogs?" said Ted.

"Dogs come from up the street,"
announced Teddy.

Ted thought, *of course they do,*
and remembered Michael.
He hadn't seen Michael for how long?
"It must be forty years," thought Ted aloud.

"What?" said Teddy.

"It must be forty years since I've seen Michael,
I wonder where he is?"

"Michael who?"

"Michael Wood, the dog next door,
up the street."

"Oh," said Teddy.

"Why do you wear that bandage?" asked Teddy.

Ted looked sadly at his bandaged wrist. "Oh, just because my paw wore out," he said.

"Like my growl wore out, I suppose," suggested Teddy, glad that Ted was not perfect.

"I suppose," said Ted still searching for a clever reply. Then he had an idea.

"It gives me a worldly look," he explained.

"What does?" demanded Teddy.

"My bandage on my worn out paw," said Ted.
"With that and me together," he went on,
"I am a Worldly Bear." He remembered
that somebody once had admired him,
and shaken him, and told him he was
a worldly bear.

"What's a worldly bear?" asked Teddy.

"One that's worldly," said Ted wisely.
He was quite content just being worldly
without having to explain what it meant —
that's part of being worldly.

"I'm an Idle Bear," said Teddy.

"I know," said Ted, "You told me so."

"Don't you want to know what an Idle is?"

"No," said Ted.

"My owner is an Idle," said Teddy ignoring Ted, "so I'm an Idle too."

Ted wished he knew what an Idle was.

And he is still thinking about it.

The bridge where
we watched the trains

Nan and Gramp's house

the summerhouse

Grandpa's
garage

single plank bridge

the   river

For Peter, with my love
S. J-P.

Susie Jenkin-Pearce

When I was a
Little Girl

HUTCHINSON

London Sydney Auckland Johannesburg

When I was a little girl I lived in the town.
But in the summer I went to the country.

My grandpa would meet me from the train.
He would take me to my aunt and uncle's,
where I shared a room with my cousin Peter.

Sometimes, we'd wake up
before it was light and creep
out of the house. We'd run
down to the lake to watch
the swans fly in at dawn...

. . . or we'd walk through the fields to the woods and look down at the village below.

Then we'd pick mushrooms that
had grown up overnight in the cowfield.

Back at the house my aunt, still sleepy, would
know the good from the bad. We ate them for
breakfast.

Sometimes, we visited Grandpa and Grandma. We'd walk across the fields and over the one-plank bridge. When it rained I was frightened to cross, for the river ran right over.

My grandparents' house smelled of roses
and lavender and geraniums. At
lunchtime Grandpa would put a bowl of
rosepetals in my place, instead of food.

Then we'd help him polish his motorbike.
We loved the garage, it smelled of sawdust and oil.

We'd have our tea in the summerhouse by the butterfly bush.

On the way home to my aunt's, we often stopped to watch the six o'clock train. The driver always waved. We watched until it was a tiny dot in the distance.

Then we'd play in the garden until
bedtime. We'd fling my uncle's top
hat into the air to try and catch bats.
We never did, though.

And every night, when we were
tucked up in bed, my aunt would kiss
us and whisper, 'I love you more than
the moon and the stars and the wide,
wide world.'

First published in 1992 by Hutchinson Children's Books
an imprint of the Random Century Group Ltd
20 Vauxhall Bridge Road, London SW1V 2SA
Random Century Australia (Pty) Ltd
20 Alfred Street, Milsons Point, Sydney, NSW 2061, Australia
Random Century New Zealand Ltd
PO Box 40-086, Glenfield, Auckland 10, New Zealand
Random Century South Africa (Pty) Ltd
PO Box 337, Bergvlei 2012, South Africa

Designed by Paul Welti
Printed in Hong Kong
Typeset by The Creative Text Partnership
in 16 point Electra J/N 37506

British Library Cataloguing in Publication Data is available.
ISBN 0 09 176359 2

the hill

the cowfield where we picked mushrooms

Peter's house

Peter's Village

Swan lak